W9-ATR-113

SAM
Is My Half Brother

By Lizi Boyd

VIKING

For Nicholas

VIKING
Published by the Penguin Group
Viking Penguin, a division of Penguin Books USA Inc.,
40 West 23rd Street, New York, New York 10010, U.S.A.
Penguin Books Ltd, 27 Wrights Lane, London W8 5TZ, England
Penguin Books Australia Ltd, Ringwood, Victoria, Australia
Penguin Books Canada Ltd, 2801 John Street, Markham, Ontario, Canada L3R 1B4
Penguin Books (N.Z.) Ltd, 182–190 Wairau Road, Auckland 10, New Zealand

Penguin Books Ltd, Registered Offices: Harmondsworth, Middlesex, England

First published in 1990 by Viking Penguin, a division of Penguin Books USA Inc.
1   2   3   4   5   6   7   8   9   10
Copyright © Lizi Boyd, 1990
All rights reserved

Library of Congress Cataloging in Publication Data
Boyd, Lizi,   Sam is my half-brother
Lizi Boyd.   p. cm.
Summary: A young girl, fearful that her newborn half brother will
get all the attention, is reassured of her father's love.
ISBN 0-670-83046-1   [1. Brothers and sisters—Fiction.   2. Babies—Fiction.
3. Stepfamilies—Fiction.]   I. Title.
PZ7.B9886Sam   1990   [E]—dc20   89-48722
Printed in Japan
Set in Goudy Old Style.

Hessie's daddy and stepmother Molly called from the hospital. "You have a baby brother named Sam! You'll meet him when you come for the summer. We love you! 'Bye."

Hessie was disappointed. "I'll ask Molly to have a baby sister next time," she thought. "But maybe I'll like Sam."

Soon school was over. Daddy came to drive Hessie to
the lake house. "Last summer there was only me.
Now there's Sam and it's *HIS* house!" thought Hessie.

When they arrived Hessie gave Molly a big hug and
asked, "Where's Sam?"

"He's sleeping," said Molly. "But we'll sneak in and peek
at him."

They went into the room next to Hessie's. Hessie
looked into the crib and said, "Wake him up so I can
say hello!" But Molly said, "Shh, sweetie, wait until
morning. You must be sleepy, too."

Hessie's old room felt good. "It's MY house, too!" she said. Suddenly she heard Sam crying. "Oh, no! I can't sleep with that awful noise!" But she covered her ears and soon fell fast asleep.

When Hessie woke up Sam was crying again. She went
to his room. His face was wrinkled and red. "He looks
mad," thought Hessie. Then Molly came in, picked up
Sam, rubbed his back, and he was quiet.

Daddy made breakfast. Molly fed Sam. She would give him a spoonful and he would spit half of it out! "Yuck!" shrieked Hessie. "I was never that PIGGY!"

Molly and Daddy made funny faces. They talked in funny voices. "I am going to talk in my REAL voice," said Hessie. But soon she was making silly faces. "Molly! Sam is laughing!" said Hessie.

Then Hessie helped Molly give Sam a bath. "His eyes look just like yours," said Molly. Hessie looked closely at Sam and asked, "Does being a half sister mean we look half-alike?"

"No, saying half is just a way of explaining that you have one parent who is the same and one who is different," said Molly.
"But it sounds silly," said Hessie. "People don't come in halves! We're whole!" Hessie and Daddy and Molly laughed.

"I want to hold him," said Hessie. Daddy put Sam in her lap. "Oh, he's so cute!" she said. But Sam began to squirm. Then he began to scream. "He doesn't like me!" yelled Hessie. "Take him, Daddy!"

In the afternoon Hessie said, "I want to go swimming." But Daddy said, "Let's work in the garden while we wait for Sam to wake up."
"But I don't want to *WAIT*!" Hessie whined.

But Hessie loved their garden. "Daddy! We have little green tomatoes!"

Finally Sam woke up. They all went down to the lake.
Hessie was so excited to see the ducks she screamed,
"Hello, ducks!" Sam began to cry. And Daddy said,
"Please don't shout. Sam's ears are new to this world."

Hessie wished she was still the only child.

One day at breakfast Hessie watched Sam as he played with his hands. "He needs something to eat, too," thought Hessie. She gave him a piece of bread.

But suddenly he began to choke. Molly yelled, "What's in his mouth?" She picked him up and pulled out the piece of bread. "Hessie, babies only eat mushy foods. Don't give him bread!"

Daddy put his arms around Hessie. "Once you were a baby, too! You cried just like Sam. Your mommy and I took care of you and rocked you, too. Now you're a big sister. You'll be able to teach Sam all sorts of things. I can't even count all the things you know how to do!"

Hessie felt better. "But when will Sam be big enough to play with me?" asked Hessie. Daddy said, "Babies grow and change every day. Next summer Sam will be walking!"

Hessie ran to the woods. She sat on her big rock and sulked. "Babies, babies, babies! There are too many rules!

You can't shout.
You can't wake them up.
They wiggle and squirm when
you hold them.
And everything is BABY this
and BABY that!
You're always waiting for the BABY!
I want to go home!"

Then Daddy found Hessie. "What's up?" he asked. "You and Molly only like me half as much as Sam because he's a baby!" Hessie said.

Hessie was happy to be grown-up. "I'm going to be
the best big sister!" she said.

The next day Molly said, "I need to go to town. Hessie, will you help Daddy take care of Sam?"

"We'll take him for a walk," said Hessie.

The bumpy dirt road made Sam giggle. But then he
began to fuss. "Why do babies always cry?" asked Hessie.
"It's their way of telling us if they're hungry or thirsty
or sleepy. I think Sam is tired," said Daddy.

"I can rock him to sleep," said Hessie. She sang, too, and soon Sam was asleep. Hessie put him in his basket.

"Daddy," said Hessie. "I can't remember being a baby."

"Well, I remember," said Daddy. "Let's look at your baby book. Here's a picture of you in your bouncy chair. And in this one you've just discovered your hands. You grabbed everything, even my hair. In this picture you're crawling! Mommy and I called you Spider because you were so fast. And here you're clapping because you had just learned to walk."

Hessie had an idea. She jumped off Daddy's lap.
"Where are you going?" asked Daddy.

"I'm going to make something," said Hessie.

When Molly came home Hessie said, "Look what I've made for Sam!" Molly and Daddy sat down and began to read the story Hessie had written under her pictures.

Hello Sam. I'm your half
sister Hessie. BUT I lOVE
ALL oF YOU!

I have two families. So
I can only live with you
half of the time.

I'm making you a book so
you will remember
being a baby.

I want Daddy to send me
pictures of you ledrning
to crawl.

When you get bigger we'll talk on the telephone.

Next summer I'll take you to my secret place in the woods.

You are really cute. But when you cry it hurts my ears!

It's o.k. You're just a little baby Sam!

And I love being your big sister!

Franklin Pierce College Library

00060063

DUE DATE

JAN. 0 2 1992			
FEB. 2 6 1992			
MAR. 0 3 1992			
OCT. 0 8 1992			
MAR. 1 1993			
MAR. 27 1995			
MAR 3 0 '97			
AUG 1 3 2007			
MAR 1 4 2012			
DEC 1 3 2012			
			Printed in USA